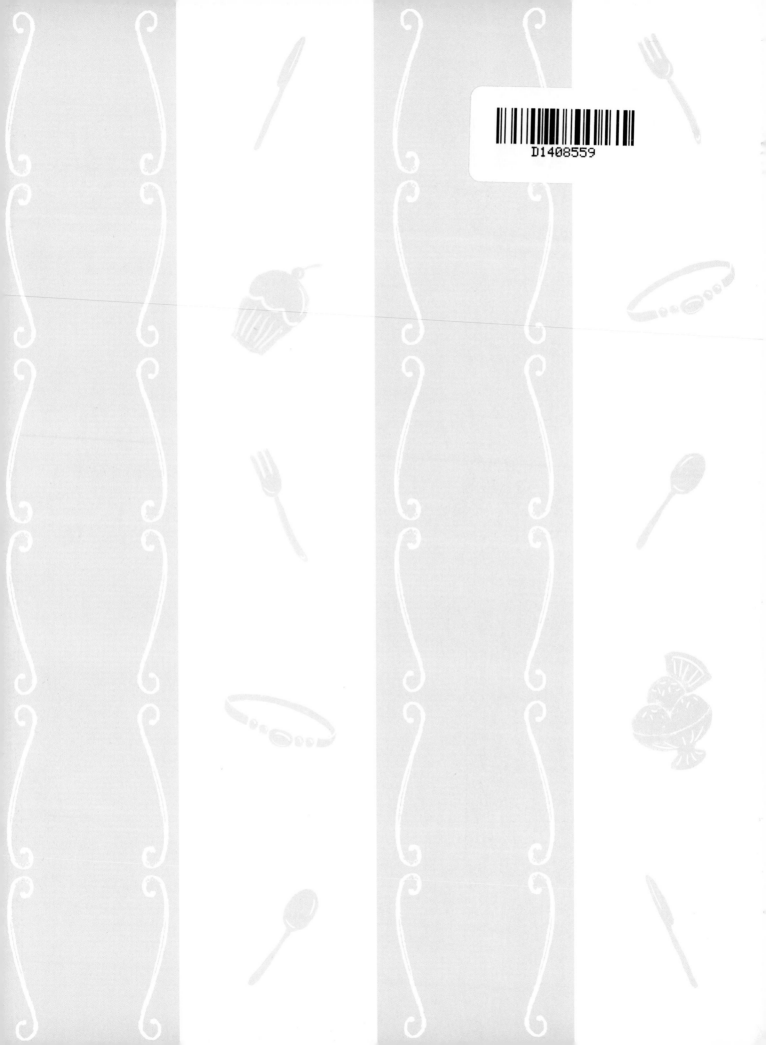

D1408559

For Penelope, Seneca, and Mama Maria —M.R.
For Isaac and Meela —G.F.

Text copyright © 2020 by Maya Rodale
Jacket art and interior illustrations copyright © 2020 by Gillian Flint

All rights reserved. Published in the United States by Rodale Kids,
an imprint of Random House Children's Books,
a division of Penguin Random House LLC, New York.

Rodale and the colophon are registered trademarks and Rodale Kids is a
trademark of Penguin Random House LLC.

Visit us on the Web! rhcbooks.com

Educators and librarians, for a variety of teaching tools, visit us at
RHTeachersLibrarians.com

Library of Congress Cataloging-in-Publication Data is available upon request.

ISBN 978-1-63565-229-1 (trade) — ISBN 978-1-63565-230-7 (ebook)

MANUFACTURED IN CHINA

10 9 8 7 6 5 4 3 2 1

First Edition

Random House Children's Books supports the First Amendment
and celebrates the right to read.

Lady Miss Penny
❧ Goes to ❧
LUNCH

By M. Rodale
Illustrated by Gillian Flint

RODALE
KiDS

New York

My name is Lady Miss Penny.
I live in the city with a girl called Milady.
We do everything together.
But my most favorite thing we do is . . .

. . . go out to eat!

Milady loves to take me out to all kinds of restaurants,
so I absolutely must be on my best behavior when we go.

And I am!

Well, mostly.

RULE #1: Always review the restaurant rules before you go out to eat!

Sometimes even Milady needs a reminder from ME, Lady Miss Penny!

RULE #2: Always WALK in a restaurant . . .

Walk to your table. If you like, you can
strut your stuff like a sassy pup!

. . . even when you really want to run.

I know it can be SO EXCITING, but
do NOT make a mad dash for a table.
This, my friends, is not the dog park.

RULE #3: Do stay in your seat . . .

Here's what to do when
you get to your seat:
SIT and STAY!

Strike a pose like this:
nose in the air, butt in the chair.
Absolutely no scampering
here and there!

. . . because dashing around is a recipe for disaster!

If you're dashing around,
your leash might trip a waiter
and make a massive mess!
Horrors!

Look, if this happens, do not try
to help clean up by licking food off
the floor. Repeat after me: EW!

RULE #4: Do wash your paws . . .

...ake a trip to the bathroom,
...e...tial to wash your paws after.
Us...oap AND water!

Most foods will need a fork and knife, a spoon,
or chopsticks. Keep your napkin on your lap,
just in case something slips. Utensils can be tricky!

. . . so you can use your fingers for finger foods!

However, one may eat French fries with one's fingers. BUT ONLY IF THOSE FINGERS ARE CLEAN. Which is why rule #4 is so very important.

RULE #5: It's okay to talk at the table . . .

Talking is fine when out to dine!
Do engage in quiet conversation
with all your pet friends at the table.

Here's what to do: use your inside voice
to say *yes please* or *no thank you* or to ask
What did you have for lunch today?

. . . but leave the barking for outside.

Here's what is not okay: barking or talking with your mouth full, or yapping or howling. For goodness' sake, do not whine!

RULE #6: It's okay to play with (quiet) toys!

If you are under the age of ten years, three months, and two weeks, you may play with toys at the table, especially if it helps you SIT and STAY.

Personally, I like to bring a bone to chew on quietly while Milady talks to her grown-up friends, but you might prefer books or crayons and paper instead.

But do resist playing with the food.

Building a tower of carrots or a pile of peas or a potato catapult is almost always a bad idea.

**RULE #7: Please stay AT the table—
not ON the table or UNDER the table . . .**

Do not go under the table, even if you really, really
want to. No matter what's going on down there!

. . . and remember, it's okay to just leave something you drop!

Speaking of staying in your seat, you might think it's helpful to skitter below the table to get something you dropped or to lick crumbs off the floor. SO TEMPTING, I KNOW.

But restrain yourself. Just leave it! A grown-up will take care of it later.

RULE #8: You don't have to like it . . .

Sometimes your food arrives and there is the most vomitous, revoltingous thing ever. It's okay to ignore it if you JUST cannot eat it!

. . . but you really should try it.

Milady taught me to try anything at least once. You might discover something totally delicious! But if you do take a bite and it truly is the most vomitous, revoltingous thing, just leave it!

If it's wrong to ask for something on the side, I don't want to be right.

RULE #9: Always use the magic words!

Never forget the magic words:
PLEASE and THANK YOU
and LADY MISS PENNY,
YOU ARE SUCH A
GOOD LITTLE DOG
(MOSTLY)!

But the most important rule of all is . . .

RULE #10: DO HAVE A GOOD TIME!

HAVE FUN, kids and kittens! Going out to eat with family and friends is one of life's great treats!

Let's review the rules!
Once more, with feeling!

1. Always review the restaurant rules.

2. Always WALK in a restaurant.

3. Always SIT and STAY in your seat.

4. Do wash your paws!

5. You may talk at the table,
   but leave the barking for outside.

6. It's okay to play with QUIET toys,
   just not your food!

7. Stay AT the table, not ON or UNDER
   the table. If you drop something, just
   leave it!

8. You don't have to like it, but you really
   should try it.

9. Always use the magic words!

10. Do have a good time!